W9-CZR-581

For Stellan, Elouan and Augustin

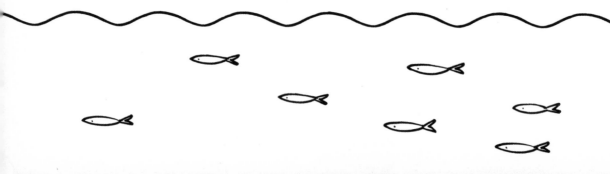

DANNY

Yann & Gwendal Le Bec

FLYING EYE BOOKS

LONDON - NEW YORK

Danny,
a happy potbellied hippopotamus,
splashed about in a swampy marsh.
When he felt in the mood for a tooth
scrub, Danny would sink to the bottom
with his mouth wide open and wait for
the cleaner fish who immediately
came in their dozens.

"Just two hours' work," said the supervisor fish, "and they'll be as good as new!"

"New, well, certainly," continued his colleague, "but with a jolly big gap in the middle."

"Well, what can you do… I wouldn't be surprised if the poor hippo lisped," replied the supervisor fish.

"True. Though you know, with a good pair of braces…"

"Yes, but I'm not a dentist, am I? It's no concern of mine."

Aghast at what he heard,
Danny ran to find his friend Steve the snake.

"Hey Steve! What do you think of my elocution?"

"Thay again?"

"Do I lisp when I speak?"

"Lithp? Whath that thuppothed to mean?"

To get a clearer picture, Steve took him to see his friends.

"Do I lisp?" asked Danny, anxiously.

"Lithp? Whath that thuppothed to mean?"
answered the choir of snakes.

"It's when you speak strangely," explained Danny.

"Ah yeth, well, you do thpeak thrangely thath for sure."

"Drats! Well, I'll just have to run into town and see a dentist then."

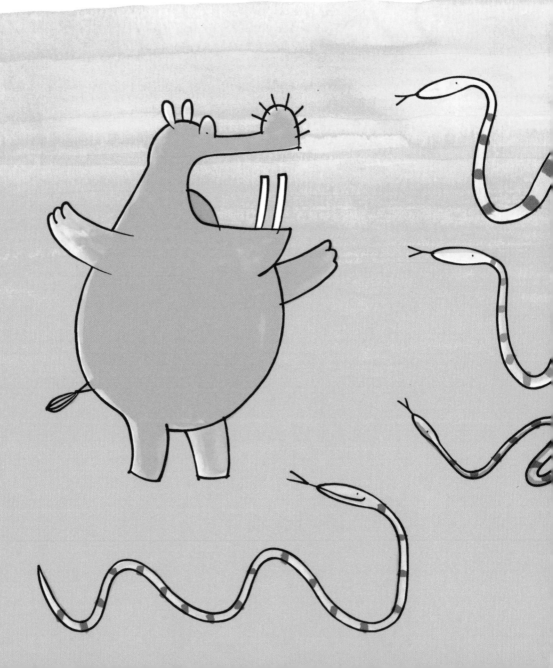

Danny couldn't wait a moment longer, so he packed his suitcase and headed for the bus into the city.

"Excuse me?" he asked a passer-by.

"You wouldn't happen to be a dentist, by any chance?

"Well, of course not."

"And you, sir?"

"Me? No, but I know someone who is.
Take the first right and you're there."

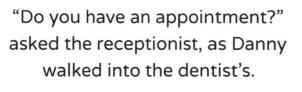

"Do you have an appointment?" asked the receptionist, as Danny walked into the dentist's.

"No, I don't," Danny replied.

"I'm sorry, Sir, you really must have an appointment."

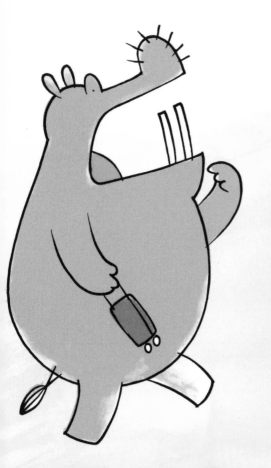

"Listen Miss, I've come very far and have a terrible lisp!"

"Alright, alright, have a seat and I'll see if we can squeeze you in," she replied.

After a long wait, the dentist was finally free to see Danny.

"Sit down, old boy. Now, what brings you here?"
the dentist asked.

"The problem is I've got this lisp," replied Danny.

"I see. Open wide. It's clean alright, but,
my dear boy, look at this jolly big gap in the middle.
You did the right thing by coming to see me."

"This man is a genius!" thought Danny.

The genius worked tirelessly all afternoon with a welder's energy and the meticulousness of a goldsmith.

"Job done, there you go!"

"Marvellouth! Doctor, I'm tho
happy I could kith you!"

And so he left the surgery happier
than he'd ever been before.

The next morning, just as
he was showing off his braces in the
middle of the swamp, a crocodile
approached him.

"Well now, what on earth is that?" the crocodile asked.

"They're bratheth. They're exthtraordinary!"

"Incredible! I must have a pair!" the crocodile exclaimed.

"Ith really very thimple – you juth have to thee an dentitht."

No sooner was the crocodile in town
than he was sitting in the dentist's chair.

"Well, old boy,
your teeth are perfect!"
exclaimed the dentist.

"Did you look all the way down, right down at the back?"

"Certainly!" replied the dentist. He leaned in for a closer look...

...so much so he tumbled into his patient's belly,
who swallowed him by sheer force of habit.

The crocodile had simply responded to his
crocodile instincts and, as it's well known, crocodiles
eat dentists. The crocodile panicked and quickly
put on some clean scrubs and called in the next patient.

"Sit down," he told the patient.
"Now, what brings you here?"

And against all odds the crocodile became an
excellent dentist. Patients disappeared from time to time,
but what can you do... a crocodile's a crocodile,
even if he is a dentist.

As for Danny, he stayed in his swamp,
always smiling and always saying,

"I muth be the happieth hippopotamuth on earth."

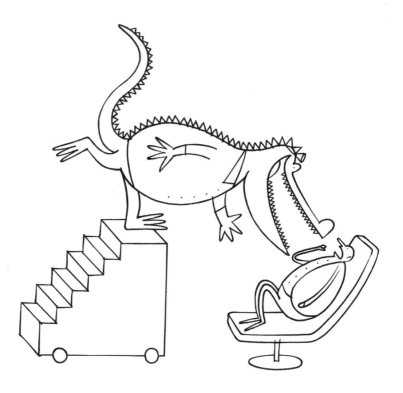

Danny is © Flying Eye Books 2014.

This is a first edition printed in 2014 by Flying Eye Books,
an imprint of Nobrow Ltd. 62 Great Eastern Street, London, EC2A 3QR.

Text and illustrations © Yann and Gwendal Le Bec 2014.
Yann and Gwendal Le Bec have asserted their right under the Copyright,
Designs and Patents Act, 1988, to be identified as the author and
illustrator of this Work.

All rights reserved. No part of this publication may be reproduced
or transmitted in any form or by any means, electronic or mechanical,
including photocopying, recording or by any information and storage
retrieval system, without prior written consent from the publisher.

Published in the US by Nobrow (US) Inc.

Printed in Belgium on FSC assured paper.
ISBN: 978-1-909263-42-0
Order from www.flyingeyebooks.com

31192020802011